-This Page Left Intentionally Not Blank, With Words-

The Hoofed Sloth Flock Presents: Campfire Stewries VOL. 1 The First Helpin'

© 2016 The Hoofed Sloth Flock

Made in USA

Written, Proofed, Formatted and also Edited by us. No, really.

Pictured left to right: El Steve, Alex Fulton and Samson Mojo

And introducing: Slops! (Cyclops Sloth) – Mascot Extraordinaire, Back cover

The Hoofed Sloth Flock is: El Steve (Steven Shatka), Alex Fulton (Alex Fulton), and Samson Mojo (Mike Schacherer).

ISBN-13: 978-0-69263-736-4

WARNING!

If any of this offends you, grammatically speaking, good.

#FlockWithUs

Contents of Table:

Chapter 1: Who Hungry?

Chapter 5: Make 'Em Stew.

Chapter 6: Settin' and Servin' and Feedin' Faces.

Chapter 7: Clean!

Chapter 8: A Nightcap, Perhaps?

<u>Preface</u>

These are the words before those words. We hope you enjoy those words after these words.

<u>Premise</u>

Groovy pals n' gals telling stories 'round the campfire; indulging in each other's stew recipes. During and throughout the entirety of these here happenings, this phenomenon is known as Campfire Stewries; from our beautiful brains to your sweet face. Stoke that fire and get lost in the wonderful world of Stewries!

*Disclaimer: Most Stew Recipes are mostly hazardous to your health

Introductions

Cats and dogs, ladies and gents, freaks and geeks, and older than pre-teen to mid-teen children (hell, anybody who has a sense of humor, for kicks, dammit): welcome to The First Helpin' of Campfire Stewries by The Hoofed Sloth Flock! This portion is brought to you by Samson Mojo. With me as usual are Alex Fulton and El Steve. We hope you enjoy something that I like to render as oddly soothing. I bid ya'll adieu for now and see you soon in the pages upon pages of Stewries.

Says Alex: "I hope you enjoy reading the stories as much as I enjoyed writing them. They represent a small slice of what I hope continues to become a tradition bigger than my own meager contributions. Thanks to everyone ever for the inspiration. Stew's on!"

"Welcome to the wonderful world of Hoofed Sloth Flock! Where up is up, down is lamp and yesterday used to be tomorrow (obviously). Join us on a marvelous literary extravaganza of stuff, and/or things. You may laugh, you may cry, you may choke to death on a small bone the very next time you satiate your poultry craving. But one certainty remains, you're about to encounter some words that make you say: Wut? Come one, come all, and enjoy that funk, that sweet, that nasty, that gushy stuff."

-Love, El Steve.

Thank!

Alex Fulton: Mom, Dad, the Hoofed Sloth Flock and You for reading.

Samson Mojo: Chick, Folks, Kin, The Program, Male and Female Brahs, Food and Drink, House, Brain, the other of them, The Hoofed Sloth Flock and You!

El Steve: Friends & Foes, Numero Uno (Moi), Dairy Products and Childish Thoughts. Special thanks to the other two-thirds of the Hoofed Sloth Flock. This would not exist without your efforts.

Um, Filler, Ya, Filler, That's It...

There's been stuff and things brought to the attention by the tension from eyes of a face to the eyes, of a face. Words have been written. They are before these ones. More are next. Here at The Hoofed Sloth Flock, we are kind (of) assholes. Be patient because coming soon, to the next page near you, is quality top-shelf low-brow scribbled hi-jinx. We make statues crumble because giggles. Hell, even the more serious one percent would muster a sensible chuckle as they caress the elevator of success past the glass ceiling. Here be s'more words. This manuscript of tom-foolery and jumbled jargon stems from galactic inlets being our ever expanding collective mind. In these crazy times where everything is seemingly bad, we offer what we dub as knowingly weird. Turn the hypno-boxes off and put your reading faces on!

Chapter 1: Who Hungry?

Samson Mojo

The Mighty F

A man. His animal. His other item. The climb from Hell is a mother.

Ugh. Not this again. Not even sure what the time would say if I ask when. Same day. Same lava boneyard. Same lava bones tearing through my intestines. I have my fanged cohort and my grappling hook. Every new time I come to, the voice tells me to escape. Is this Hell? Fuck if I know. I can't stick around to find out because the all-consuming darkness creeps near. But somehow I'm lava and bone resistant, save for the forced-entry pressure. So at least I got that going for me.

My name is Donald David Donovanson, but you can call me not late for dinner. With me as always is my weird looking but functional fur friend Borage Shikai, the bulldog shibe. Every day I shoot my grappling hook to the next level. Every day the darkness chases me. I'm able to make it through the random-things-that-stab-you corridor and surpass the mighty inside-out arena. I can hit the high notes because the sound hole. The visions I see are of non-darkness and minus lava bones. End-result appears to be an endless waterslide, making it's way downtown.

My depth-perception skills are my downfall. That and vertigo is a bitch when everything is spinning. Spinning. Round and round. There are things to fight wherever I proceed, you can picture them however gruesome and know that I can also think of some encapsulating horrific shit. Every day or night I get dismembered as they partition my body parts so. The darkness consumes as I once again am left hung out to dry. It's never tomorrow. It is always today. I rebirth like an overflowing toilet. Once again, I emerge from that same origin with lava pouring from my face.

Slewed and Brewed Bruised Moose Goo Stew:

Feeds Whomever Gets Most

Ingredients:

- 1 Large Moose or 2 Not As Large Meeses.
- 3-5 Gallons of Nearby Animal Fluids
- 1 Tree Sap
- 1 Handful of Finely Grounded Spices
- 3 Mystery Plants
- Stardust
- 7 Gallons of Rain Water
- 1 Cauldron
- Indefinite Pieces of Firewood
- 1 Huge Fucking Stickknife

Cooking and Then Eventually Feeding Faces:

(Note: Have all the ingredients how it's said, don't be an asshole.)

- Wait for a rainy day then go find moose or two individual meeses
- Use stickknife for sick twenty hit combo
- Skin moose/meeses; wear fur for victory
- Save hooves and half of antlers
- Put cauldron on indefinite pieces of firewood
- Fill cauldron is with 3-5 gallons of nearby animal fluids and 7 gallons of rain water
- Wait for boil; throw hooves and half of antlers in cauldron
- Pour tree sap, sprinkle spices and stardust and mystery plants within
- Throw moose/meeses in after chopped
- Wait for the smell
- Stir thrice with stickknife
- Consume from hands whilst crouched over cauldron
* For dietary purposes, ingest into preferred cavity

Alex Fulton

Icewater and Angels

Inventory-

Contents of Pockets:

- Car Keys
- Receipt from store for 2 bananas, chocolate sauce, vanilla ice cream
- Asthma Inhaler
- Business card from donut store visited at breakfast
- Cell Phone
- Wallet

Contents of Wallet:

- Driver's License
- VISA Card
- Movie ticket stub
- ATM/Debit Card
- $47.89 in cash

Sneakers squeaking on freshly waxed floors as the doors of the mall are flung open with the rising sun. The faceless people scuttle by, caught in the torrent of time.

I slink by; a pair of rusty legs, hoping to be as unnoticed as possible and simultaneously hoping to never be forgotten.

Loud sounds and bright lights. Empty promises of eternal delights.

The fake food from the vendors and the familiar and unchangeable smell creates hunger. I saunter past and admire jeans that promise a better life and gadgets that insist on carrying the answers to the deepest of questions.

I spend another paycheck and fill my house with more crap I don't want. I need the comfort that the routine of the purchase gives me.

I live.

Icewater from the filtered fridge and ceramic angels, provide life and security. These things keep me safe.

I live.

In a box.

No amount of icewater or angels will put out the fire that burns me.

Uncle Duncan's Country-Fried Stew

- Biscuits

- Gravy

- Corn off the cob

- Boneless Fried Chicken

Cut the chicken into small pieces and mix in with gravy and corn off the cob. Dip the biscuits in the mixture.

El Steve

Poke-Her

He was always a gambler. From a tender age, Damien always possessed a devil may care attitude. Well mannered, yet an affinity for chaos seemed to envelop him since birth. As the years passed however, these same traits that defined him eventually betrayed him. Damien now found himself planted squarely at the end of the long dick of the law. Being a man of notable intellect and drive, Damien put in the time, payed the fines and eventually scratched his way back to the surface of acceptable standing with the judicial system. He had unknowingly discovered the secret to success, and his eventual demise: conformity. Society shall prevail!

As luck would have it Damien soon scored himself a respectful job with benefits, which eventually afforded him the opportunity to purchase his very own slice of American Pie. A modest house in the suburbs with a picket fence, and a yellow Labrador in the backyard as the cherry on top. This newfound lifestyle soon attracted an attractive female companion that was loyal, cooked and cleaned. He soon found himself in an awkward position for a man of questionable background. Possessing not just a socially acceptable, but a socially desirable lifestyle. On paper and in theory this should have pleased a man who had squandered opportunity, good women, material objects and wealth in the past.

"Welp, its Groundhog day again," he found himself muttering almost ritualistically as he set his morning alarm the night before. Six days a week, six AM. His wife found it humorous and Damien always played it off coolly as if it were his intent. Day in, day out, the grind, 401k, morning coffee, mediocre monogamous sex, vitamins, electric bill. Stuff stuff, things things.

Wash, rinse, and repeat, till you die. The pure unadulterated monotony of it all plagued Damien for the better portion of a decade. Anything he used to find pleasure in as a younger man was not an option, his jimmies had not been rustled the slightest in as long as he could remember. Damien had been choking the life out of himself to fit into a society he suddenly realized he was never meant to be a part of.

After a particularly in particular work day, rather than the usual commute home Damien found himself at a used car lot. "That one," pointing towards a candy red Corvette. Casually trading in his trusted work truck, he now found himself speeding off towards the sunset and the interstate.

Riding shotgun was his long forgotten pal Jack D, and what a reunion it was! Once the scalding amber nectar first caressed his lips, till the last glistening drop, was pure unadulterated bliss. Fifth deep and blaring heavy 80's metal, he genuinely hadn't felt such elation in years. He felt the blood hotly coursing through dilated veins, felt the rush, the thrill repressed in the name of normalcy. As the lines grew blurrier, the music grew louder, the pedal fell further and his thoughts grew clearer. Even thru the alcohol induced brain fog, he knew this feeling was unsustainable. In one last act of defiance, one last fuck you to the status quo, this was his escape. Cranking the wheel sharply to the right he hit the perfectly pitched berm, tached out in sixth gear. Now air born for what could have been a brief eternity, Damien found himself grinning ear to ear, betting on an afterlife he was never entirely sold on. But then again, he was always a gambler.

Poke-Her Stew:

PROCURE THE FOLLOWING ITEMS:

- One soiled bathtub
- One Erlenmeyer flask
- Pre-civil war era oar
- Two farthings
- Access to homeless man/woman
- Grandmas Lederhosen

INGREDIENTS:

- Four large possum
- Brick of bullion
- Batter
- Imitation spam
- Tears from Tibetan yak

DIRECTIONS:

- Pummel possum(s) with Pre civil war era oar into a pulpish substance

- Toss bouillon cube into not very clean tub with an unnecessarily loud grunt
- Pay homeless man/woman two farthings to strip bare and enter not very clean tub
- Strain Yak tears and batter thru Grandmas Lederhosen over the head of homeless man/woman
- Rub down homeless man/woman with imitation spam 'till you can see reflection in the greasy sheen
- Place oar in the hands of homeless man/woman and demand they paddle ferociously until stew becomes frothy.

*If said homeless man/woman is reluctant to paddle threaten with extreme sodomy

SERVING SUGGESTION:

Horde around tub with 14 of your closest pals and pig out trough style.

Lick homeless man/woman clean for a gritty dessert-like something

Alex Fulton

Grandpa

It seemed like I had been waiting in the car for hours when suddenly the announcement on the P.A. declared that the flight had been cancelled and wouldn't be arriving until tomorrow. Irrecoverable time, forever lost, it frustrated me to no end, however, I knew that this change of plans could potentially be advantageous to me; Grandpa wouldn't be here for another day, after all.

Not to say that I didn't love Grandpa Horace, it was just that he had a way of going about things in life that made him feel the need to control every little thing, all the god damned time.

I was free for the night and it was a rare occurrence that I didn't have class or work so I felt a little bit of excitement that I could do whatever I wanted. I chewed on my nails for a minute, a really disgusting habit that I had picked up somewhere along the course of my life.

Just to make sure that what I'd heard on the P.A. wasn't just wishful thinking, I went inside the terminal and checked the board and sure enough, the flight had been delayed for the night.

I could pretty much do anything I wanted. I lit up a cigarette as I walked back towards my car trying to decide where to go or what to do. I looked through the names and phone numbers stored in my cell phone and nobody seemed worth calling or making plans with.

I got back in my car and sat there for a minute; I didn't want to waste a bunch of gas driving around, I really needed to decide what my next course of action would be.

The morning sun woke me up initially, followed by the sound of birds and in the distance, a leaf blower. Suddenly all the commotion of a busy morning at the airport faded back into my ears.

It took me a minute but I realized I had fallen asleep in my car the whole night and I didn't end up doing shit with my free time, except for smoking a cigarette and biting my nails.

I looked at my phone to see the time and saw that I had a few missed calls and a voicemail from Grandpa. I checked the voicemail, but it wasn't Grandpa, it was the voice of my Aunt; her sobs and hysteria caused the words to almost make no sense, but I understood the message; Grandpa wasn't coming today, or tomorrow, or the next day, or ever again.

While I was in my selfish, fucked up world, my Grandpa died. I could have died myself and part of me did that day.

I watched the planes come in and my heart broke more and more as I knew he wouldn't be on any of them.

Grandpa's Great Gravy Stew:

- Plenty of gravy

- Lots of gumption

- A bit of patience

- Biscuits

Instructions:

Prepare the gravy and using gumption AND patience, dip biscuits into.

Chapter 2: Journey to the Marketplace!

El Steve

Kid Stuff

When you're small, you want to be big, grow tall and do the big things big people do. As a small person I recall how much I was looking forward to being able to see the top of the fridge. Upon reaching the requisite height, one could argue this disappointment as foreshadowing. It was mostly dust and a couple mouse turds.

Ohh the possibilities were endless, dreams of riches, recognition, maybe becoming a professional athlete. Delusions of grandeur aren't classified as a mental condition when you're small. In the transition from small to tall, the more you grow the further to fall. There's a whole lot more to trip over, likely no four leaf clover.

Life is gonna give it to you, just bend on over. Now that I'm tall, what I would give to be small. No regret, no debt, nobody to judge on what you have, or haven't done yet. Try your best to stay true, to what made you before you became you. Grow tall; think small, you will fall. Get back up, shock them all.

Kid Stew:

INGREDIENTS:

- Four quarts white vinegar
- Three pounds Fun Dip
- Dash of Leprechaun funk
- One Pork Butt (whole)

DIRECTIONS:

- Sport them hobo gloves
- Grab Pork Butt (whole) firmly, but not so tight as to bruise the tender loins
- Stick pork Butt (whole) 7-8 times in the same spot as to open a hole in the whole pork Butt (whole)
- Pour vinegar in the fresh still warm (friction) hole
- Dry rub the whole pork Butt (whole) starting from the hole working outwards
- Spread leprechaun funk around rim of pork Butt (whole) hole

SERVING SUGGESTION:

Toss that big bitch in a big Ass bowl and tongue punch it ferociously 'till your sick twisted hunger is satiated

Alex Fulton

Baseballs

Billy had been staring at his dinner for over 5 minutes. With a gag and a grimace, he pushed the plate as far away from him as he possibly could. "What's wrong son? It's baseballs, your favorite!" Billy's dad said as his glasses bounced on his nose between bites of meat soaked in some sort of greasy red sauce.

"Dad, I know what baseballs is! I'm never eating this again!" Billy said as he ran into his bedroom and slammed the door. Billy's dad, ever-mindful of saving a buck and Billy, always curious about the endeavors his father took, one day saw his dad's beat-up 1982 Isuzu pick-up truck parked behind the local animal spay-and-neuter clinic.

With horror Billy saw his dad, knee-deep in the dumpster behind the clinic with a bloody grocery sack, whistling with joy as he scooped in the discarded dog testicles. Billy, suddenly threw up and remained hidden in the bushes until his father drove away, vowing never to eat "baseballs" ever again. Oh, and if you couldn't fucking guess, I was Billy.

The End

Baseball Stew:

- Meatballs
- Tomato Sauce
- Corn off the cob

INSTRUCTIONS:

Mix all the goodies in a big old pot and serve around a fire while telling the guests that they too are enjoying dog balls.

Samson Mojo

The Whistler

Noise plagues the local merchants. With eyes peeled, they take heed for possible misdeeds, yet the whistler in the dark lurks within earshot.

My Allah-given name is Amanar Adarange, but everybody calls me Steve. Or "Hey, you." The Bakos have such a way with words depending on pigment. Alas, I digress, for a bigger debacle must be addressed. As the new breed scatters, the power man scans the cover of the night. The power man fails to see The Whistler with no light.

The Whistler is one or many. He or she is they or them. The Whistler is a protocol code. It does not take a rocket surgeon to recognize The Whistler trying to triangulate more than one coordinate. The merchants, the power, the townsfolk and others stay silent watching the universe unfold.

Human nature, not Ma nature, nurtures functions deeper than a cognitive surface. Ma nature, on the other hand, not human nature, nurtures the ideal of nature doing whatever the hell it wants, because its Ma nature and no F's are given. Not now, not ever. One non-biased example is the duck (scientific-Latin-word-for-duck-imus). What better type of duck than the everyday ones that sound like they are laughing? What a quack up!

What do the laughing ducks and The Whistler have in common? From dusk to dawn answers that question. From dusk, the air fills with shrillness thanks to The Whistler. To dawn, the laughing ducks are near maniacal with their chorus of chanting chortling as if they were charmed by a chump coaxing them with handfuls of chunks of crumbs. Here's where it gets tricky, like a sicky gnar skate move on Halloween. The speculation of the aforementioned person, persons or people (maybe peoples); as well as the multitude of hysterical bills share a commonality.

Something is foul akin a trouble afoot. A webbed foot. A foot away from feet. A fleet with feet fleet moments by way of lunar shadows. The man in the moon manipulates women and men. The Whistler proceeds to go berserker, which in turn deals damage in the worst laughing ducking way. Because of moon burn, weirdness creeps between wax and wane. And if you remain, The Whistler and laughing ducks are one in the same.

Banana Powder Chowder Extravaganza!

Appealing to a large family of seven parents

- A Bunch of Bunches of Bananas
- Hella Handfuls of Banana Chips
- Those Cheap Ass Banana Scratch N Sniff Stickers

- 4 Gallon Jug of Banana Juice
- Pound of Banana Pudding Powder/Pound of Banana Jell-O Powder
- Crock Pot Half Full of Banana Pudding
- Crock Pot Half Full of Banana Jell-O
- Beloved Banana Stylee Cauldron
- Firewood[2]
- Gorilla Arms Taking Place of Yours

In All Seriousness, No Monkey Business

- Ready All Banana Variations
- Pour Liquid Banana Anything in to Cauldron
- Boil Tough

SLAM. OTHER. BANANA. WHAT. NOT. IN. CAULDRON.

- Beat Chest
- Jump Rope with For Some Reason Gorilla Arms
- Donkey Kong Cauldron
- Go Bananas!!!

Note: Potassium

Chapter 3: Behold: Glorious Inventory for Which We Shall Feast Upon!

El Steve

Cletus' 'Beetus

Good ol' boy Cleetus reeked of the 'beetus since he was but a wee fetus. Mother bled from her head in a double wide shed from a blow from tiny Uncle Ned, we must be fed!! The feeding was breeding in between the sheen of a gristle missile straight to the eye.

Aye aye fry guy get in my gut, out the butt down a lengthy ladder. Quite the splatter of matter, which matters all the more when landed on your front door. Oh now what's in store, in store for you?

Losing your shoes in Cleetus poos, now past the knees, rising till you can't breathe! Lungs full to bursting, tongue thirsting for anything but, the shit-shake that now constitutes most your body weight.

You're showing, you're growing in girth, preparing for birth of the being within. Cleetus the 'beetus fetus now greets us; you're born again and again. Your putrid offspring shall thrive.

'Beetus Stew:

PROCURE THE FOLLOWING ITEMS:

- E-40 Album
- Stunna Shades
- Copious amounts of malt liquor
- Glock 19
- 160-175 rounds of ammunition
- Burlap sack
- Ingredients
- Hella fuckin' shit

DIRECTIONS:

- Pop that Forty Water joint in your most bumpinest system
- Sport them Stunnas!
- Get twisted off that Malt pimp
- Toss hella fuckin' shit in that burlap
- Pump every last round you got thru that bitch to agitate that shit whilst showing the block, you don't play

SERVING SUGGESTION:

Gather the homies and get down with the get down, fuck around.

Samson Mojo

The Trials of Miles and Giles

There are many adventures. Life does this. Either right directly to the facial collection of people, or perhaps served on a velvety cloud-like pillow. Life can be good, life can be bad, but life will always be weird. Today's subjects are Miles and Giles. Here we go.

The many quests and journeys have been in increments of various degrees of stress, pressure, pleasure, but not treasure. There's never ever treasure, sadly. By all means, these experiences are trials. These are the trials of Miles and Giles.

In addition to frowns, there are various grunts of excitement, and you can bet your ass there are smiles. Don't bet your ass though, that would be weird. And look silly. The asses of those asses being Miles and Giles have been in hot water, on thin ice, not out of the woods yet, padded, kicked, kissed, handed to and inside out above and beyond. The consensus of velocity per hour is forty miles for Giles and Miles.

Many a traveled path have been by way of sea, sky and skies, trails, back roads, backgrounds, underground, down towns and by later version of stagecoach. Otherwise, vessels have been not all metal, but all over and all-encompassing, very moving. The only mode of travel missing thus far is the portal, which is the missing link of the missing piece of my heart.

All is well, because the forty mile an hour portal compiles Miles and Giles greatly in piles of files within aisles of tiles. The styles of a portal going forty miles an hour for mere mortals (being Miles and Giles) can only end in sore sorted spores sporting skin stretching akin to a busted accordion.

Besides the in depth description of the lack of portals or perhaps the lack of using portals, Miles and Giles have traversed under the healing sun and under fire of father and son. Hemispheres semi smear cultures' angst among our global sphere. As luck, fate, destiny or the universe would have it, Miles and Giles's styles is a bit beguiled in that throughout their trials, they have been only so glib, but mostly great because of their seemingly fresh slab of gab.

Circumstances warrant trials. Miles and Giles very vary with their perhaps smiles there. They're spare with anticipating fear. Any emotion is rationed for the rationale of the commotion in motion. Passive assertive has been the standard unit of action. A case by case basis has been the main constant in the trials of Miles and Giles. The end result per hour has been forty miles.

Ice Cream Cake Pie Soup Stew:

- 1 Coldron (Stew Cauldron for Cold Stew)
- 1 No Firewood
- 1 Ice Cream Truck with Contents minus Driver (but in a Good Way)
- Ice Cream Sammiches in Proximity
- 1 Big Hands
- 1 Large Candy Cane that is a Real Cane
- A Winning Attitude

HERE'S THE WHAT:

- Dangle Ice Cream Truck over Coldron. With Big Hands.
- Mash with Real Cane Candy Cane.
- Gather Ice Cream Sammiches in Proximity. With Big Hands.
- Probably Unwrap them Sammiches. With Big Hands.
- Slam, Place, Set and Put Said Sammiches in Coldron. With Big Hands.
- Using Big Hands, Grasp Real Cane Candy Cane and Engage in Hurricane Activity.
- Watch as Hurricane Action Produces Ice Cream Cake Pie Soup Stew.
- You know what to do next. With Big Hands.

Alex Fulton

A Squirrel's Life

The bright lights came out of nowhere and swerved to avoid me.

The sound of the beast roaring past startled me.

The pebbles creaked under my feet as I ran to safety.

The fog swallows the moon glow's shadows.

I scampered back into the darkness, safe yet again.

I heard another beast roar past and dared cross again.

The road was cold as I darted across, but...

...I didn't quite make it. The black tires smashed me in an instant.

Just another dead squirrel on the highway.

Squirrel Stew:

- 1 Squirrel
- 2 Cups of Chicken broth
- 1 Cup Mixed Veggies
- 1/2 Cup Asphalt
- Clean and brown the squirrel
- Mix all the ingredients up
- Stew over fire until nice and cooked

Chapter 4: Adventure to Back Home-ness.

Samson Mojo

Places

There are places placed covering space in space. Things make for people to embrace these spaces in places on this place in space. A gathering of faces in particular various places engage in the formulation of graces at copious crossroads and places. Faces placed in places in spaces in space's place. Place is earth. Face from birth. Spaces plumb with girth.

Everywhere is here or there for faces places far and near. With that kind of placement begets a warm, glowing atmosphere. With open arms and bright eyes, lent ears are bountiful and plentiful. Plenty of bounty to gather then rather slather on the wayside of every townie in all their splendor of each county. Be mindful of the toxic teeth chattering about.

Presently placed is this juxtaposition to show the mission and expose the wishing vision. Enlightened smiles with broad shoulders ever expand only to retract those open to receive. In the face place within space is encased the flowing aura which is embraced.

Amidst anything stagnant prevails a progressive positive feat. This featured feat feels of fate. Fate floats unbridled to destiny's doors. Destiny answers fate. Fate's plate is served in a place, to a face. The mystery dessert that is destiny is only visible when the eye is ready to see. (*Author's note: I just turned over the notepad paper I'm rough-drafting on. I'm wearing a white shirt.*)

As the universe unfolds into fruition, places cascade from space's spaces. Faces faced to traces of grace are no longer displaced. Blurry becomes a less static-esque flurry. The worry and fury scurry like a flock of hoofed sloths. A flock of hoofed sloths are most definitely furry. Shedding hoofed sloth pelts are very good clothes of which to dispose. The righteous universe becomes exposed. Ladies and gentlemen...this case is closed.

Condiments Stew:

(Always Being a Weird Batch, this Compliments You!)
Mixes well, ethnically culturally speaking

Step 1: Store. Chain or Mom N Pop; makes no biggie or diff.
Lettered Number B: Double or nothing desired liquid anything you used to cover food for stew for you.
III: Purchase from shopkeep:
4: Cauldron.
Five: Fire W's.
Upside Down 9: Crazy straws.
Five + 2: You better be absolutely sure.

-All the sudden, you are back at camp-

- Red hot cauldron awaits sauceness

- Make crazy straw staff

- Dump food sauce altogether now

- Do the crazy straw staff stir!

- Slurp sauce stew.

- Leave no remains

- Unless for sharing.

- Sharing is cool

That's it.

Alex Fulton

Roadkill

Driving down the highway with the roads dark and dull I see another. I pull over and pop the trunk, dragging out the soaked bag, I scoop up the smashed armadillo and plop it into the bag. I drive on.

A desolate stretch with the stars and my thoughts, I feel the familiar thump and stop the car, a grin spreading across my face. I deposit the skunk into the bag and drive on. I can smell the death in the trunk, like rotten cheese and the ocean, my nostrils breathe it in and I smile, thankful my time hasn't come yet where I'll be scooped up and plopped into a moist and dark bag. I drive on into the night, needing the roadkill to remind me of my life.

Roadkill Stew:

- Various dead animal meat.
- Beef broth, enough to soak up the meat.
- Ketchup.
- Brown the meat and plop it into the beef broth, serve with ketchup.

El Steve

Mom's Spaghetti

I'd been a bag of shit for as long as I could remember. Selfish as a three toed sloth in a finger factory. Meaner than a grizz in spring. Nobody told me what to do, and even if they had, I sure as shit wouldn't hear it. Humans perceived me well enough, a likeable fellow to most. Somewhat ill-tempered at times, paired with an affinity for violence, but fair. Yet deep within the confines this soft, grey matter was harbored such malice, a malcontent for my complacency and lack of action.

Do I feel as I am timeless, as if there is a sort of supernatural phenomena surrounding me providing infinite chance? Much thought, much too much thought. Or not enough perhaps? The absolute matrix of possibilities surrounding my altogether finite being, and utter lack of motivation to explore them has rendered me defenseless, thus spiraling deep into the confines of a lifestyle paralysis.

Creativity, what is that? Physical prowess on the decline. Individualism? Naw, I'll just fit in. What. The. Fuck. Let me be me, let you be you.

We've only got one shot, mom's spaghetti. Never forget, although don't try too hard to remember either. I beg of you, for the love of Mtn. Dew and NASCAR. Please never, ever, never ever, swear on your baby brother Trevor, ever forget. Mom's spaghetti.

Mom's Spaghetti Stew:

PROCURE THE FOLLOWING ITEMS:
- Filthy, nasty Pornog
- Marlon Brando look-alike
- Scalpel

INGREDIENTS:
- Brown rice
- Black beans
- Yellow corn
- White bread

DIRECTIONS:
- Feed Marlon Brando lookalike ample portions of each ingredient
- Turn on filthy pornog to excite Marlon Brando lookalike to the point of bursting to expedite the Scientific processes
- Cut Marlon Brando lookalike from bow to stern thus spilling the most politically correct concoction ever concocted ending racism as we know it

SERVING SUGGESTION:
Invite one friend of every race, color and creed over to tell tales of your respective peoples and post about how progressive and tolerant you arc on FB.

*if you lack chums of every race, color and creed paint them the colors of the missing peoples and continue as instructed.

Alex Fulton

The Dream Life

"Baby, sugar bear, can we go to the Hostess Store for dinner again?" She pleaded, her begging eyes sinking deep beyond the dollar-bill stank and gross-sex humility of the motel room in which they made their home. Her few remaining teeth and the rot-black-yellow stumps in her mouth needed sugar the least but wanted it the most.

When she got no response from the still drug-slumbered Horace for a moment she poked him and he awoke, startled. "What's that, honey doll?" He asked, still sleepy. His own body odors from the various drugs taken and the several truck-stop scum-screws and freeway overpass bridge-fucks gave him an inhuman and almost fungal-like smell. He let out a wet-sounding fart, surely adding another stain to his already soiled and yellowed underpants.

They had only been in the motel for a few days but it was already a fucking disgusting rat's nest of filth and a breeding ground for Staph and fungal infections, it didn't matter though, the sores up and down their wasted bodies already contained the pus-draining filth of MRSA, their unwashed genitals had more than enough yeast to make a beer, the toilet already had shit-stains, there was hair all over the sink, their crap belongings; filthy

44

clothes, various, half-abandoned soda cups and chip bags containing cigarette butts and loogies were all over the place.

He opened his eyes and said, "You know it. I'm-a get me some of them Lemon Pies for fruit and vitamins." He let out a belch, the smells of cheap-beer and partially digested generic cheese-puffs added to the symphony of stench in their rat-hole motel. "Ohhh!" She let out a squeal of joy as the fat bounced on her pig-like body.

She turned the TV on and there were the Kardashians , their lives different, but unbeknownst to her simple-mind, no less filthy than her own existence. He lit a half-smoked cigarette, courtesy of somebody abandoning it in the lobby ashtray. He let out another fart, a small puddle of shit slid out, causing his butthole to stick to his underwear. He let out a cheerful sigh. "God; I fucking love America" He said. "This really is the dream life."

All-American Red, White and Blue Stew:

- Corn Chips
- Cheese Puffs
- 1 Pack of Cigarettes
- 1 Bottle of Vodka
- 1 Pack of Chocolate Mini-Donuts

Instructions:

Mix it all up in a big pot and simmer for 1-2 hours. Be sure to enjoy with Sister-Mom and Uncle-Dad.

Chapter 5: Make 'em Stew

Alex Fulton

Butthole Stew

All of our parents in the neighborhood were acting weird all summer long. Parents are always weird, but there was something different this past summer. Something just wasn't quite right.

Teddy LaCroix's dad, Chester, who undisputedly had the best yard on our block and was winner of the Tri County's Annual Lawn Lord Award the last four years in a row, suddenly started to ignore his yard and eventually the weeds took over and the grass died. It was a strange sight-seeing what was once a picture-perfect yard totally messed up and thrashed.

Marcus Bakker's parents hadn't been seen outside in weeks, the only thing that let me know they were still alive were the late nights when I'd hear their garage door open, followed by their minivan driving away and returning sometime in the middle of the night before the sun came up again.

Cubby Schmidt's dad, Oscar, normally the sweetest and

friendliest guy we knew, had suddenly quit his job and had abandoned his suits for nothing but a pair of pair of bicycle shorts, exposing his pale, fat and hairy body with the tight shorts leaving nothing to the imagination. When we would walk by his house he would glare at us and squat, the alcohol-liquid-cornnut piss/shit diarrhea spraying out of his ass like a broken fire hydrant as he hissed at us.

Eventually I couldn't take it anymore and my curiosities got the best of me. Having failed earlier that afternoon in my pleas for Cubby to come with me, he gave me a grenade to protect myself; he figured it was the least he could do. I didn't think I would have any real use for it, but I took it as more of a talisman if anything.

I waited until the night was still and quiet and fought off the sleep as I lay in bed waiting until I knew it would be safe to sneak out. I finally got out of bed and slowly opened the window to my bedroom and quietly slunk down the street. Faintly in the fields at the bottom of the street of the neighborhood I could hear a muffled sound.

Curiosity overcoming me yet again, I walked towards the field and my eyes filled with horror; there, in the middle of the field, all the parents were encircled around a big fire with a giant pot on it. Swaying back and forth with their arms outstretched in front of them they tonelessly chanted "Arooba, Adooba, A-Butthole Stew, Arooba Day Doo, A-Butthole Stew." The pattern never wavered, they just kept repeating this over and over and over and to my horror, I could suddenly smell the funk of what must have been thousands of buttholes simmering away, the disgusting filth which would have undoubtedly been served to placate the appetites of such sadistic fucks such as the aforementioned psycho parents and, unbeknownst to myself and to my friends, passed off as some kind of stew at the annual Fourth of July neighborhood Potluck, which was a mere few days away.

Well, I wasn't going to allow such things to occur and as I chucked the grenade that Cubby stole from his old man a sadistic smile crept on my face watching my parents, my friend's parents and a huge pot of butthole stew explode in a giant inferno. "Well, that was a shitty way to go out." I said, chuckling as my 12-year old and now-orphaned lips cursed. It sure felt great to be free.

The (Almost) End

Whoa, there!

Note, if a story about a homicidal 12 year old murdering his even more sadistic and evil parents and friends' parents makes you feel offended, why did you read a story called "Butthole Stew" in the first place?

The (Real) End

Ehrmegherd A Recipe!

Yes, you too can make your very own butthole stew! Here's how:

Ingredients:

- 1 Can of pork and beans
- 1 Hot Dog cut into small pieces
- 1 spoonful of corn off the cob

Directions:

Mix all the ingredients and simmer slowly until warm.
Enjoy knowing you just ate a dish called "Butthole Stew."
Try the real thing next time with buttholes and dog shit!

El Steve

Fart Box

Fuck this fart box. As far back as I could remember father would lock me in this putrid crate. Albeit the years have passed, I am now 32. In the not so distant distance the clamor of his fellow, heathenish, snarling, back hair-a-glistening kinsmen invaded my ears like a rebel force. The fart foyer, as dubbed by yours truly in my adolescent years, was full to capacity as told by the creaking floorboards above.

The feast had begun. Platters of broccoli, 37 bean casserole, an array of cheese that would make any Swiss native proud, and all types of heinous, prune related atrocities were consumed at an alarming rate. This wasn't my first rodeo cowboys, yet rather than assuming the usual fetal pose, quivering like a frostbitten lemur I remained cool as Freddie Mercury. Ya know, before the AIDS. I passed the time playing a few levels of candy crush and snapping a few cleverly angled selfies to negate the king's share of my soft, shitty physique. No service in the fart box, offline activity shall suffice.

Why the calm demeanor you ask? Am I not about to have the stank of many middle aged, rot gut imbecilic nincompoops embedded in my nostrils? Nope. Father goes first, he always does. I heard him grunt deeply as he penetrated himself with the hose leading to my domain. He was obviously unaware that during my mandatory weekly cleaning of the pigpen they used as a clubhouse I had made a few, let's say changes.

I barely heard the onslaught of flatulence being evacuated in my direction. My excitement level was near frenzy. He was finished, game time. I heard a slight scream as he went for his dismount. The reverse barbs must be holding I thought to myself. I heard the commotion above escalate. Must. Be. Patient. Let the barbs dig into his tender flesh; let the old man suffer as I had so oft.

Show time, with a devilish glimmer in my eye I hastily flipped the switch. For the first time ever I was so very proud of my industrial strength, ultra-extreme duty shop vac that had consumed decades of unspeakable excrement. "MADE IN THE USA, BITCH!!" I screamed at the top of my lungs as I heard the entrails beginning their decent. Silence, then utter horror and chaos above erupted as I showered with the insides of my father, for the very, last, time.

Stank Stew:

PROCURE THE FOLLOWING ITEMS:

- A partridge in a pear tree
- Sling
- Ball bearing
- Nutrient extracting juicer

INGREDIENTS:

- Partridge
- Pears

DIRECTIONS:

- Place ball bearing in sling
- Sling ball bearing at partridge, mortally wounding said partridge
- Shake pear tree real hard and gather dropped pears
- Throw deceased partridge and pears into nutrient extracting juicer
- Extract those nutes!!!

SERVING SUGGESTION:

Gulp down that mix Hombre, you're now the last item in the
Christmas classic,
12 Days of Christmas!!!

Samson Mojo

Cacophonous Color Castle

Most strongholds mean to keep intruders out. Being usually dark and overly raucous, numerous citadels crave chaos. There is a keep kept away in the forest, on the mountain. For only during the most overcast moments within the murkiest of murks appears the dormant yet vivid acropolis in its entire vibrant hubbub splendor. This rare sight is seldom sought, but is cherished still and all. Off in a remote location apart from societies' abrasive ways awaits the cacophonous color castle.

Music! Perhaps a jig! Perhaps further jigs! Jovial carousing in the name of what's right because of what's left. Because of the canvassed mope stemming from the not so greater gullet, people-kind must embrace itself as one commencing to shake feel in unity. Best place for rhythm to groove must be the pigment fort with the tunes. Fortunately for anyone who gives a hoot, our castle makes no terms on which to enter. The only elusive factor our castle casts is the whereabouts of the path en route to the woodland within the midst of the pinnacle's crest.

Because fun and happy are subjective, entryway is only accessible by way of hot air balloon, locomotive, space capsule returning from orbit or fourteenth century catapult. These strangish but seemingly entertaining methods of traverse are mainly to prepare eventual attendees for what could be their best moments. The qualifier is this: doth laughter, chatter, knee-slapping and more than likely more than one story of various exciting rooms whet your whistle? If yes, locate a vehicle to transport you for the last ride you'll ever take for the final trip you'll ever have to make. If no, not so much, or meh be your response, look at the aforementioned question, because what?

Now, we are on our way. Unless, no was your answer. Is it yes yet? Does this say yes? Remaining humorous is the ticket to keeping an open mind and entry to our mostly loud, but also quiet, bright and dark visually hidden available spot. The cacophonous color castle is that and isn't that. At the same time! This very real dream place is bouncy to the music of your choice, but sturdy to maintain enough levels of sanity. This eventual pleasant experience is within reach for those who have squabbled with life and then woke up through various and particular peculiar trials and tribbs. There must be some adverse expansion from the familiar humdrum routine. Danger isn't necessarily necessary, but something vast must shake the brain awake. The hard-headed ones will have minimal assistance, but being stubborn, advancing forward with their horns lowered, they can take the gloves off and learn as fast as stupidity permits. The cacophonous color castle accepts eager learners who can forgo the evil intent of anything selfish.

Time is of the mind. Society produces deadlines and every community follows. The transition from structured material anything to the most peaceful free-for-all within reason is a shift of attitude slightly beyond mental capacity of the so-called normal. Will you, the public, surrender ideals of ranking within various statuses and borders that separate humanity from being one human race? This is the last sentence.

Missing Stew:

*This stew is missing

Alex Fulton

Thanksgiving

I woke up early to the sound of the rain pattering on the roof and windows. The bird was thawed and I wasn't even awake as I stuffed it and threw it in the oven. I had my coffee on the porch as the rain came down. I prepped the other things and helped myself to more coffee and a handful of M&M's. The phone rang, Corey and the family couldn't make it; the snowfall up in the mountains had forced them to turn around. We wished each other well and got off the phone.

Donald called next. The twins had the flu so they couldn't make it. I wasn't sure what to do with all this food I was making but I had already crossed the Rubicon; the food was already being cooked and had to be completed. I realized I was out of cigarettes and decided to talk a quick run in the rain to the corner liquor store, hoping they would still be open.

Luckily the store was open and would be all day. Suddenly, I felt really bad that the store was going to be open all day, but my sympathies could only go so far as I had worked countless holidays the last several years, in fact this was the first Thanksgiving I had off in like twelve years.

Walking back home the rain started to come down really hard so I was glad I got the smokes when I did. On my walk back I saw a couple of weirdos trying to get shelter under a couple of boxes they were propped under. The boxes were already soggy and useless and it was pathetic seeing them like that, smoking old cigarette butts with filthy clothes under shitty old cardboard in the rain, my heart gave out to the poor bastards and it was with that sympathy that I did the unthinkable; I offered them over for Thanksgiving dinner. Worst. Mistake. Ever. We'll get to that soon enough, though.

We got walked towards my house. I could smell the booze, piss and regret all over them and I tried my best to ignore it. The wet of the rain made the smell even worse but I soldiered on. We got to my place and they oohed and aahed and my little piece of shit house. It was the most praise I'd ever gotten on my domicile before.

I made careful note of the greedy looks on their eyes, making sure to inventorize all my stuff, the chance of them trying to pocket something was high and I was already regretting inviting them over for Thanksgiving.

Their soiled fingerless gloves touched pictures, paintings and other sentimental effects which I had stored in my house, forever tarnished by their filth. No amount of Lysol would take away the stain which they had permanently affixed to said items. I took a deep breath and continued the Thanksgiving Dinner preparations.

We all sat around the table, the bums took their beanies off and solemnly bowed their heads. I lowered my head and began to say grace when I felt something hot smack into my head, I looked up and saw one of the bums had flung some mashed potatoes at my face.

Instantly, I got up, I was so pissed at this point. I flung the table up, spilling the food everywhere and trashing the table, the contents spilled in their direction and they reeled backwards out of their chairs and crashed onto the linoleum floor in the dining room. I stood over one of them and kicked him in the side of the ribs, he groaned as the other guy reached in his pocket, likely to pull out a knife or something, I jumped over and stomped his hand, still in his pocket and felt the bones crack like old fried chicken pieces.

I felt a fist crash into the side of my face as the other bum sucker punched me. I fell to the ground and they both got up and encircled me and began to kick me. Knowing unconsciousness was impending, I willed myself to gather my strength and get up.

Unbelievably, I succeeded and was back on my feet, fighting my way out of the brawl that had ensued in my dining room, on Thanksgiving, with two bums. It wasn't long before I had taken control of the situation and, brandishing the turkey, I threw it at one of the bums and knocked him out cold. I then took the pan that once contained gravy and bonked the other bum over the head, sending him to the floor.

Like a cheesy movie I said out loud, "Time to take out the

trash;" and then I grabbed them one at a time and tossed them out my front door, which sent them flying down the stairs into the street. I got back into my house, surveyed the mess and awaited the bums to take their revenge on me and my house. They never did.

Thanksgiving Stew:

- 1 Thanksgiving Dinner

Take all the fixins for a usual Thanksgiving Dinner and smash it all up into a pot and stew it up, making sure to toss the pot in the air before serving.

Chapter 6: Settin' and Servin' and Feedin' Faces.

El Steve

Tape Worm

A parasite, a pest. An entity that destroys and consumes the rest. Narrow mind, near sight, a once noble journey turned to plight. Abominable darkness engulfing light. Past the point of no return, past the pain, past the burn. No second thought, no concern. Lost all connection with Mother Earth, de-evolution observed as human birth. Exalted eyes fall on such chaos below. An uninspired, and quite expired marionette show. Allow the charade, or time to go?

Fuck this shit. Curtain call bitch. Raining hell, so precise, complete. Death like a martini, extra neat. Before the ages were dark, more like stone. When we were smart, not a phone. Basic function obstruction, a requisite for utter destruction. Time has reset, erase your kin, predating history to where we begin. Been there before, now here again. Play to lose, one simply cannot win.

Check mate. Too late to negate, can't undo what's done. Fate set in motion, web already spun. Our sanctuary compromised, we've failed the test. Trial by fire, rid the pest.

Human Stew:

PROCURE THE FOLLOWING ITEMS:

- Old timey boxing gloves
- Gorilla strength
- Taped episodes of Nancy Grace
- 17 Gallon Hat

INGREDIENTS:

- Boiled sloth egg
- Many handfuls of Nesquik ™
- All the sauce

DIRECTIONS:

- Toss freshly boiled sloth egg and all the sauce into 17 gallon hat
- Put on old timey boxing gloves
- Throw many boxing glove handfuls of Nesquik ™ into the mix
- Watch taped episode(s) of Nancy Grace
- Try to bear thru the next 30+ minutes of torture without becoming homicidal
- Use gorilla strength and go HAM beating the mix into frothy purée

SERVING SUGGESTION:

Grub down bruh

Samson Mojo

Forward Movement

As the dark smudge surfaces, the stubborn nerves still grasp the onyx nebula. Each nerve signals danger to the blotched void. The platform opens, expanding a theme of release in the most non-come hitherto attitude.

The throne awaits, however, this typically inaccessible super special seat is available to all. Shocking to the few snowflakes, which are oblivious yet also unaware of anything present; for wholesome positivity grows as dullness shines. Lumpy mounds of filth can be deceiving without proper light.

What used to be a mud ball rolling about is now a glowing orb. Glowing orb floats innocuously, only to flourish. Banter spewed from locales is absorbed then perhaps discarded. Nuggets and tokens and gems beam ever so graciously onward to the keepsake. The orb becomes expansive with affluence. Greatness exudes radiantly as all surrounding environs benefit. Neglect becomes a fading stain. The past is a shadow of itself, currently not scathing the here and the now. Behold what an evident glimpse the future stores!

Our previously filthy and bleak spot is now a compound of greatness, awaiting the masses. As the pending promise prognosticates, high hopes are never dashed under the guise of presumption. For in lieu of punctuated demand, a genuine certainty engrosses the previous complexities of the unknown. An absolute fluid strength prevails over toxic mush. Wholeness proliferates from a breeding ground of disparage.

Existence is no longer imagined reality. The planes of striving effort meet approval in plumes exiting from the nodding mitochondrion. Joy and wealth advertise in a most binding fashion. Onlookers sense the comfortable draw, which is possible providing a condition, perhaps. A negotiable timing is the necessary pathway. The life span of this passage just is. What happens next really depends on them.

Double Double Cheeseburger Stew:

- Double Double(s?)
- A Cauldron Boosted from a Witch's Hive
- Meat Discs
- Bottles of Yum Yum Sauce

- Spoons, a Shovel and a Ladle and Bowls
- Firewood from Mother Nature
- Pals

The Soups all have Lid Tabs ('Murica!)

- You or you and your pals,
- in no order at all,
- unwrap and open,
- make the drop,
- so many bubbles,
- stirring...
- stirring...
- stirring...
- not stirring,
- ladle time!

Once everyone has their bowlful,

commence in spoon to face goodness.

If cheeseburgers are tasting like multiplied,

this stew is for you!

Alex Fulton

Honkeytonk Trailerpark Blues

Well, I've got those Honkeytonk Trailerpark Thunderclap blues again. The roof of the trailer (actually, a fifth-wheel) is leaking and sagging in, ready to dump moldy old rainwater (and staph infection) all over the floor, which is also rotting out too. I had to put an old piece of wood by the bathroom because its feeling like it's going to break right through from all the sewage rot.

There's a weird brownish-red looking substance all over the walls in the shower. It looks like old blood-cum. I hope it isn't. The minute I open the bathroom, my eyes are obviously horrified but it's my nostrils that instantly try to close and my stomach that wants to instantly wretch all the food and sodey pop out all over the place from the shit-mold-piss-egg-fish-rot smell. It's the worst smell I've ever smelled and I feel light headed and dizzy, and not just from the lack of stability from the failed shocks and rotten tires; it's the fucking smell.

If I had a computer or electricity, I could probably get the Wi-Fi signal from the neighbor's but I'm not so lucky. Good thing the food bank gave out a free chocolate cake for the holidays. No one is coming over so I won't have to clean the place up.

Honkeytonk Trailerpark Thunderclap Stew:

- 1 cup of water
- 1 stick of butter
- 1 pinch of salt
- 1 hot dog
- 1 Half-Cup of cooked
  macaroni noodles

Combine all the ingredients and serve when hot. Eat, then cry.

Chapter 7: Clean!

El Steve's for Now Last Hoorah?

*For the remainder of this, The First Helpin' of Campfire Stewries by The Hoofed Sloth Flock Writing Crew, El Steve (the author currently known as Steven), has taken a bow and will be on indefinite hiatus due to stuff about things in his homeland of Whereverthefuckistan. He may or may not be number one on the charts, but he is surely number one in our hearts.

Legend has it he sends his deepest and most heart-feltestness from the innards of him black heart, the depths of he soul and the bottom half of his balls. He may be gallivanting with unsavory women, he may be nursing small Ethiopian children back to health from his supple teat. Yet we can assure you, with the absolute utmost insured assurances that El Steve shall return, galloping from the sun-kissed horizon, bronzed skin glistening, back to the flock then back to you for future helpins' of: Campfire Stewries by The Hoofed Sloth Flock.*

No tears, only dreams.

Alex Fulton

Stephenson

He started his car. The familiar hesitation as the car moaned back into life, and his relief as his prayers for it to start one more time were answered. He bonked his head, "SMACK!", as he got out of the car to scrape the frost on the windshield; he was already running late as it was. He merely escaped death as he narrowly avoided the umpteenth pile-up this week, another shitty driver causing calamity for the innocent and ill-prepared at quick decision stopping.

He tolerated the bullshit of another day at the office. Another day of "Stephenson, I need 10 copies of this, stat!" or "Stephenson, ring up those numbers on report 1432-39-3939 for me, ASAP!" or even worse, "Stephenson, Mr. Summers needs to see you in his office immediately."

He cringed as another pigeon from the rooftops of the building he worked in sent a high-velocity shit onto his head as he walked to the bench to eat his lunch. He gagged as he realized, halfway into his lunch, that the sandwich he'd made post-haste in the early darkness of dawn had moldy bread. That and the pudding cup had opened and mixed in with his watery carrots.

He blushed as urine splashed the front of his trousers mid-piss in the men's urinal and walked out back to his desk hoping nobody noticed. He sarcastically laughed as he noticed another dent on his car as he left his job, surviving another day.

He cursed as his tire blew out on the freeway and groaned as the tow-truck driver gave him the bill. He shrieked as he heard one of the neighborhood kids send a baseball through his window, shattering the glass and breaking a picture of his mother.

He waved his hands in agony as he burned the frozen pizza he had planned to make for his dinner. He screamed as he slipped in the shower as he was shaving, slashing his face and sending blood down the drain. He yelped as he stubbed his toe getting into bed and said, "Hey, it could be worse."

Stephenson's Savory Stew:

- Carrots, cubed
- Onions, diced
- Beef, browned and cubed
- Flour, water, other stuff to make stew broth
- Shredded mozzarella cheese
- Tortilla chips
- Instructions:
- Stew up all the ingredients except for the cheese and chips.

When the stew is done, throw in some chips, top with cheese and enjoy.

Samson Mojo

Forensic Future

No! People scream. Robot criminals flee. Bananas are flying about. Presently, the future is stuff. Among the living, there's also things. Robot bananas enter workforces, possibly as detectives! The revolutionary progression of society births utter chaos. Cow puns no longer run rampant, because the mood. In the United Kingdom of the World, peace is scarce. Humans lose rights as inanimate objects expand their cognitive reasoning further. The past was exceedingly different, but the present future proves quite differently.

The walls have eyes and ears, because if they're screens, they aren't walls. How's it possible for technology and other stuff that is things to be living? Science, chemistry, mathematics, society and global warming had the perfect ingredients to spawn the unthinkable. A madman mastermind plus schematics, blueprints and various beakers in addition to other components produce this. It is impossible for anybody to be thoroughly evil, because he sleeps and eats like everybody else. His name is Wilbur, and because his name is Wilbur, he was molded from bitter discouragement and his brains. The future holds no place for a madman mastermind carrying the title of Wilbur; name changes have been outlawed. You give a brainy smarty outlaw reject like Wilbur no chance to save face via name change, shit goes down.

Besides the name Wilbur, the only thing his parents left him is a place with lots of space; the space place. Wilbur is learned in the ways ranging from how to stuff to the vast arena of things within things formulating further stuff. From early on, there has been an accumulation of one thing here to some stuff there, to some more stuff and things later. Glowing, beeping and digital items of computation consisting of electrodes are stowed away as neatly as Wilbur's name is plain, in their proper place. After segments and sections of electronics are fulfilled, produce and livestock must be gathered, for juncture be like the crux (time is of the essence). It is quite amusing to proctor Wilbur rummaging about through various junkyards, locked laboratories and then as a normal shopper at the local grocer for items. Wilbur's moral compass is a bit skewed considering he'll either purchase or steal produce or technology, or by doing the exact opposite listed on the next sentence. Wilbur carries the odd tendency to snarf or acquire practical application or biology (there are plenty of words to expand on the topic of stuff, and of things).

For days turning into weeks turning into months turning into years and then decades most likely, Wilbur uses science in a mechanical way to concoct a most unnecessary evil. A bunch of bananas here, a chicken coop with a barbed-wire electric fence there, a mallet, and a catheter (possibly with the attachments: people, animals, other stuff, maybe probably machinery). All of these items (grabbed from their appropriate places, by Jove), are in a larger piece of hi-tech machinery that have various see-through compartments, various secret compartments and such. Next to that larger machine is another larger machine with, you guessed it, other stuff and things: a laser, four various monkeys and some really cool space glasses! As things connect with stuff next to other things within stuff, Wilbur is going to grasp really large cords, connect them and then do it over again. Next, switches will be switched, levers will be pulled, those wheels with the knobs attached will be twisted the wrong way and then the right way.

Following those procedures are additional methods, auxiliary modus operandi, ancillary formulae, and supplemental systems to test, analyze, scrutinize, probe and prod to ensure future operations. These future operations, eventually taking place in the future, lead us back to earlier about people screaming and bananas flying all over the place. Because of Wilbur's parent's neglect in choosing his name (based off of whomever), crime from digitized bananas or otherwise takes place in society. Nobody sees it coming, the motives are never how they used to be because stuff and things begets stuff and also things. The genome has been apportioned amongst everything else besides humans, making the future more ridiculous because of the animation of variables. Potatoes now have actual eyes, legs make tables and chairs trot down the street; literal goings on be afoot steady. Law enforcement must stick with the growing trend, and expand and extend the long arm into uncharted terror territories.

The public is not so private anymore; people can't use cars unless they have a car's full consent. The same goes for anything else used by anybody else: permission must be granted, or no deal. This is happening in the future because in the past, Wilbur could not change his name. Wilbur grouses to himself "I will make everything so unfathomable, that the universe will collapse." The produce monster whistles to summon the laughing ducks that it is now time. Clothing forms barricades as any livestock assimilates with any nearby wireless computation devices. Statues use billboards to surf from sea to shining sea for tricks. This new anarchy is not an overthrow of the government, no. This new way is the ultimate expression of all freedom. People living in harmony with robots and live furniture. Food kids participating alongside goat and people kids. All because of Wilbur being that guy. Aliens like what they see now. Maybe it is our turn. Our turn to play. And to laugh. To Smile. Bye.

Digital Stew:

#Impossible

Chapter 8: A Nightcap, Perhaps?

Alex Fulton & Samson Mojo

Ned's Needs

The morning dew clung to his lungs and he coughed the sleep out of his brain. Still yawning, he slowly rose out of bed. The grave of slumber lying dormant for another day. He lumbered into his clean, cold and lonely kitchen. The fridge growled mockingly, as though it was notifying the other appliances and suggesting he was lonely and alone. Only machines know if they are evil. His house had become the extraterrestrial hub. Otherworldly beings have vastness beyond our human psyche. Such as, giving utensils brains. When stuff can think, the living must panic. They can't because they don't even know that they don't even know.

Wide-eyed, alert and with a racing heart, the paranoia of his existence had returned just as the last of the sleep wore off, the final memento of peace that his "awake life" would afford him was the fart that didn't end up being moist and underpant-stainy. Now, several hand-scrubbings, aversions, phobias and deep-dark thoughts perpetuated the paranoid loneliness of his pathetic existence. The phones listen, the television set is ever watchful. Even the light bulbs have eyes. This test at these coordinates the prep for the alien invasion or perhaps the onslaught of the midget army. This is all tentative, considering how things can change in an instant.

Then, the doorbell rings, sending him nearly sprawling to the floor, luckily catching himself at the last minute, just as the newspaper plops through the mail slot in the door, yet another daily occurrence, but a terrifying occurrence nonetheless. "How can a newspaper make entry if he has the controlling switch button?" Ascending onward and beyond to lunacy makes him ponder the abstract. To not trust machines is safe because of the mirrors. Mechanical smiles are the discourse because they short circuit with double vision. Such mastery overlooks man's creation. Aliens are bastards in their arrogance. Humans aren't mass stupidity, but how else would the midget army know? This requires peanut butter.

The depth and warmth of peanut butter in sammiches, with oatmeal, or plain out the jar with a spoon, was, has been and will be the recurrent saving grace. Peanut butter judges not. Peanut butter only wishes to fulfill. Peanut Butter, slathered about, protects from the potential onslaught of midget aliens. The hub is neither vulnerable nor impenetrable. Ned separates brain dumb from wisdom. The floor has eyes.

His family, long departed now, had long suffered under Ned's needs and the constant paranoia he inflicted upon himself, and by proxy, those around him. He retreated from society and lived inside of his head. His appliances and gadgets were his new friends and family and would also serve as judge, jury and executioner to his conscience. Whence surrounded by solidarity, Ned gets quite the inkling for quiet loudness. By Ned's needs, this must be accompanied by a soft, warmly glowing blanket. This cannot last forever because Ned needs nourishing necessities. The local merchant knows Ned and makes available nocturnal hours once a month so Ned can be under the impression he isn't subject to ridicule; even though Ned isn't subject to ridicule. The neighbors and other community members give lee-way to Ned because they understand and they also think Ned is silly.

The neighbors wait until Ned is far and safely tucked away from their ears, or so they think; Ned knows their secret meetings and societies dedicated to his demise. Ned thinks they don't know he knows, but Ned knows alright, rest assured, Roger, over and out. Ned shrieks as the neighbor's lawnmower fires up, sending more grass and insects to their death. Thankfully, Ned sighs with relief knowing they haven't gotten him under their blades yet. Maybe tomorrow, maybe in ten minutes, maybe in a year, but not yet.

The lawnmower is part midget alien, part big brother. Ned's big brother became machine. His joints, bones, nerves and eyes pieced together with midget alien spawn makes for one hell of an aerodynamic panoramic altering apparatus. This shit is hot;

I mean Ned is oblivious to its weapon capabilities. Ned's needs are bigger than Ned. The world needs Ned. Ned and his landscaping gizmo of DESTRUCTION. Ned unknowingly will embark on a journey. Ned needs new shoes. Off to the local emporium for Ned's needs.

As Ned cruises in his shabbily disguised lawnmower, the neighborhood comes alive from pet noises and birds flying about. These animals sense a scent beyond their normal capacity. Either they scatter or stare quietly as animals usually don't and Ned advances further, gathering a following of support from the local town's beasts. He then gets the will to leave his lawnmower and gets in his car to congregate elsewhere. His time in town is spent timidly tense as he tenaciously tries to accomplish tasks as quickly as possible. He doesn't realize that his wallet is still at home on his dresser and finally finds out as he's in the food court about to pay for his lunch. Ned needs nourishment.

Defeated, dejected and depressed, Ned heads home. He makes another peanut butter sandwich and glares angrily at his wallet, almost blaming it for his mall food-less woes. Ned stumbles in his always-clean and freshly waxed kitchen floor and stubs his toe, causing momentary panic followed by a deep spell of anger, Ned needs a nap. Unable to sleep, Ned rests in bed and begins to think deep thoughts, what exactly does Ned need? He wonders this and considers his possessions and his obsessions and decides they go hand-in-hand, what it really came down to was food, water, shelter, entertainment, companionship and stimulation, a decent job, some pizzas, his apartment and book, movie and record collection would suffice, other than that, Ned needed nothing.

As Ned drifts off to sleep in bed, rattling off only his desires for just himself in his head, conscious and subconscious blend in reality's stead. The midget aliens' observation of earth's only hero has come to a close. Because of his laziness and not giving a fuck, the world becomes one giant midget alien engulfing Ned in all his narcissistic ways, followed by the rest of the shitty people on earth. The midget aliens move to the next planet that nobody will ever know what it's called because of Ned and his small and narrow self-absorbed needs.

Stew Stew:

The usual stew recipe then procedure is a list and then another list of a recipe and a procedure. The protocol is to do some crazy shit with a cauldron, firewood, pals and various pieces of equipment. This formality has been the Campfire Stewries tradition for as long as The Hoofed Sloth Flock have been about. Without you, the reader(s) being as open-minded as you, the reader(s) are, we would not have felt so inclined to spew our jargon amongst. It is time for you, you and also you to join us in what will be the most best stew for you brought to you by The Hoofed Sloth Flock. Here is the premise, the rest is up to you: have all the stew you can muster from your cerebral cortex vortex. Then put all that stew in to our trusty cauldron on top the firewood. The rest is up to you!

Alex Fulton

The Turnip Man

Across a dusty road, over a hill and..... wait a minute, that's not right. Over a grassy hill, across a dusty road, past a meadow....damn, that's still not right. Anyways, once upon a time there was a town and in this town there was a man and in this man was a brain and in this brain was an idea and this idea really wasn't very good, so he gave up on it and continued to push the cart with the onions and turnips he was selling.

"Onions! Turnips!" the man shouted as he came into the market district of town. All kinds of wares from all corners of the known world filled the man's eyes. Various spices and scents filled his nose, furthering his curiosity on the exotic locations from which they came. Woven rugs of the finest variety, clothes of the rarest cloth and musical instruments of the strangest and unknown kind all passed the man's sights as he navigated the creaky wooden cart down the road.

He finally found a place to set his cart and sell his wares; nestled towards the end of the district and far away from the main hubbub of the patrons, the man was going to have an even harder time selling his onions and turnips than usual and business usually wasn't very good to begin with anyways. The man sighed and braced himself for a long day.

His day wasn't long as he slept through it and awoke as the sun was going down and having sold no onions or turnips. His face was covered in drool and his right arm was numb with sleep as he'd been sleeping on it for the last few hours. He quickly got up to make sure his cart, onions and turnips were still ok. He was relieved that they hadn't been molested.

Unsure of what to do and a bit panicked from a fruitless day, he began the long trek back towards the small cottage where he lived. He didn't go far when the axle on his cart broke, which caused the walls of the cart holding the turnips and onions to break, which then caused the turnips and onions to spill all over the road.

"Oh no!" He cried as he scampered to grab the tumbling turnips and orbiting onions. Unbeknownst to him, he slipped on one of the onions and crashed down hard on his head, sending him back to sleep yet again. By the time he awoke it was early morning and the remnants of the cart were nowhere to be found. His head, still throbbing, ached for more sleep but he fought the urge and slowly rose.

Ashamed of the sight of his bumped head and stolen cart, he gathered what turnips and onions he could and stuffed his pockets with the few choice ones that he could fit. When he finally made it back to his cottage he was hardly surprised to see that it had burned to the ground. Still, he couldn't help but laugh a little as the life he had worked so hard for so long for had gone up in smoke in the course of a short day.

He trudged along, towards the woods where he figured he would gather more wood to rebuild his cottage. Having no ax would make it difficult to get any good lumber, but he knew he could make do with some fallen branches and twigs for the time being; winter had just left and was still long away and he felt that he would worry about that another time.

He made his way into the dark woods and allowed his eyes adjust before going too far in. He started gathering the various herbs and spices that littered the floors of the lush and lively forest. He had been going a short distance when he heard the slight murmur of human voices not too far from where he stood.

Straining his ears, he could make out what they were saying. "Damn fine onions, but what wretched turnips!" A low and gravelly voice said. "Right. But all free!" Another voice said between bites. They both started cackling and the man spying began to realize that these were the thieves of his cart. It was no splendid or special cart, in fact it was on it's last legs, er wheels, but it was all that he had and he really needed it to sell his turnips and onions.

Trying as best as he could to be quiet he still messed up and accidently stepped on a branch, it's snap startling both himself as well as the two strangers. Scampering into the darkness as quickly as he could, he felt a rock smack against his already sore head. Feeling great anger overcome him for the first time in his life, he suddenly turned around to face the rock-thrower.

Letting out a guttural and animalistic scream, he grabbed the man by the face and threw his knee into it with all of his might. The man instantly fell lifelessly to the ground, the other of the bandits saw this sight and pulled his hatchet out and came charging.

The man ducked the swift swing of the bandit's frantic hatchet and knocked him to the ground. He then grabbed the hatchet and quickly ended the threat of the bandit. He also noticed the man had a carrot and a potato. He grabbed these things and suddenly noticed the fire and the empty pot sitting atop it.

Flash forward to the man butchering the bandits and cooking them up in a stew with the onions, turnips, herbs, spices, carrot and potato and I reckon you'll understand where the story goes.

Simple Stew:

Ingredients:

- 1 pounds boneless beef sirloin steak, cut into 1-inch cubes
- 2 tablespoons oil, divided
- 1.5 cups water
- 2 Turnips, Chopped
- 2 Onions, Chopped
- 1 Potato, Chopped
- 1 Carrot, Chopped
- 2 Celery Stalks, Chopped
- Various Herbs and Spices

Directions:

- 10 mins Prep time 20 mins Cook time
- Heat 2 tablespoons oil in large pot. Add beef; brown on all sides.
- Stir in Various Herbs, spices and water. Add vegetables; bring to boil. Reduce heat; cover and simmer until vegetables are tender.

Samson Mojo

Bill's Bills

Here we have an introduction paragraph consisting of sentences. Here are some more words to make another sentence. This is the third sentence. By this time, enough words have been jotted down on a canvas for type (digital or otherwise), making a fourth sentence. And wouldn't you know it? This one and that previous sentence just made more sentences! This introduction is looking pretty damn complete. This is Bill's bills.

Bill is a simple man with simple taste. The skill of Bill however, is quite the thrill to the numerous taste buds of strangers who travel near and far to the wonderful eatery, The Pepper Mill. Bill's grills skills have caught the attention of food critics and gluttons, young and old alike. What was once a survival skill and a hobby has blossomed in to a dangling enticement which has instilled something fierce and insatiable. Bill's skill with the vehicle that is grill produces a ginormous endeavor in which people would kill. Imagine cartoon food and then imagine eating cartoon food. If you cannot imagine those two things to imagine, stop reading this because you are no fun.

Bill loves to feed the patrons whom flood The Pepper Mill. The Pepper Mill is so very dear to Bill. Outside of The

Pepper Mill is where Bill's personality and character spill. Life is not the problem, nor is there an issue. The only thing we may call a minor setback or inconvenience stemming from Bill's skills is the perhaps negotiable, but ultimately unavoidable bills of Bill. Bill's bills: oh, how they mount. Utilities. Power. Water. Trash. Gas. Gas. Probably another gas. Food. Cell phone. Telephone. Various maintenance (health (physical, social, mental and spiritual), car and house). Any missing bills that which are Bill's bills will be brought to Bill's attention, causing further frills.

The question coursing through Bill's skull is "why does life cost money?" Followed by, "why does life need stuff?" Because Bill's favorite pastime is being more than one thing to more than one person, his inner conflicts and meagerly silly logic both remain swirling around his dome. "These sure are some questions, I bet people are hungry." Bill is very fortunate get away from himself to kill it on the grill with his skill. Eight to twelve hour shifts simplify these grandiose thoughts. The culinary thrill is an enchantment still to Bill.

As long as Bill remains on the grill at The Pepper Mill, his skills won't transform immediately into bills. Bill is quite content not looking at a bill. Bill's boss Phil obliges Bill's will to exercise Bill's skills. The cycle continues onward and upward. There will always be a Bill, there will always be bills. There will always be the constant of Bill's bills; until the sun explodes or whatever.

Neighborhood Stew:

Your chance to shine!

Hopefully you haven't pissed off the locally local neighbors.

Have the required amount of firewood and your, our trusty cauldron.

Get one or more than one ingredient(s) from each neighbor.

Don't steal them, that's dumb.

- Get spoon.
- Gather neighbors for later.

  -The Then to Now Process!-

- Any Liquid from Neighbors First.
- The Other Stuff from Them Next.
- If Spoon is Small Medium, Attach to Larger Large Spoon.
- Listen, Baby.
- Ain't No Mountain High, Ain't No Valley Low.
- Indulge with Local Neighbors and Serve 'Em Up However.

Notes:

#FlockWithUs